10598258

Dedicated to
Peter Newell,
Creator of The Hole Book

THE ARTWORK WAS DONE
USING MIXED MEDIA AND
COLLAGE ON KRAFT PAPER

No part of this publication may be reproduced in whole
or in part, or stored in a retrieval system, or transmitted in any form,
or by any means, electronic, mechanical, photocopying,
recording, or otherwise, without written permission of the
publisher. For information regarding permission, write
to Viking Penguin, a division of Penguin Putnam Inc.,
345 Hudson Street, New York, NY 10014.
ISBN 0-590-63188-8
Copyright © 1997 by Simms Taback.
All rights reserved.
Published by Scholastic Inc., 555 Broadway, New York, NY 10012,
by arrangement with Viking Penguin, a division of Penguin Putnam Inc.
SCHOLASTIC and associated logos are trademarks and/or
registered trademarks of Scholastic Inc.

12 11 10 9 8 7 6 5 4 3 2   89/9 0 1 2 3 1 0
First Scholastic printing, September 1998
Printed in Mexico

THERE WAS AN OLD LADY WHO SWALLOWED A FLY

Simms Taback

SCHOLASTIC INC.
New York London Toronto Auckland Sydney

OLD LADY
SWALLOWS FLY

30 years — that the $4 billion
may be too small to compen-
them adequately, a Federal
that the $4 billion

who swallowed a fly.

I don't

know

why

SPIDER'S SOUP

SUPPER **RECIPE:**
1 FLY, 1 HORNET, 2 WASPS
AND 1/2 CATERPILLAR
SAUTÉ IN WORM JUICE UNTIL
DONE AND SERVE

who swallowed a spider

That wiggled and jiggled

There was an old lady who swallowed a bird.

She swallowed the **bird** to catch the spider.

She swallowed the spider to catch the fly.

I don't know why she swallowed the fly.

Perhaps she'll die.

she'll leave us high and dry.

There was an old lady who swallowed a Cat.

she swallowed the **dog** to catch the **cat.**

she swallowed the **cat** to catch the **bird.**

she swallowed the **bird** to catch the **spider.**

she swallowed the spider

to catch the **fly.**

I don't

know why

she swallowed the fly.

Perhaps she'll die.

there's a tear in my eye.

THERE WAS AN OLD LADY WHO SWALLOWED A FLY, a favorite American
folk poem, was first heard in the United States in the 1940's.
Several different versions from Georgia, Colorado and Ohio were collected for
Hoosier Folklore (Dec. 1947), but its true author remains unknown.